The Portal in the Park

Find the wealth inside yourself

Story by Cricket Casey
Songs and audio book performed by
Grandmaster Melle Mel/Featuring Lady Gaga

More Books for Young Readers
More Books
PO Box 1225. New York, NY 10008. USA

More Books Press P.O. Box 1225, New York, New York 10008

Cover art created by David Combs.
Cover and book designed by Yvonne Liao.
Music produced by Joey Mekkah; project recorded at Black Solaris Studios in NYC.
Edited by Cliff Carle; assistant editor: Rita Cody.
Illustrated by Allison Casey.

The Portal in the Park/Cricket Casey and Grandmaster Melle Mel.
(The Portal in the Park 1)
Sequel: The Biorhythm Academy.
Summary: A boy accidently falls through a portal and takes a scary journey into another dimension peopled by horrible creatures who attempt to destroy his spirit.

1. Creatures — Fiction. 2. Children — Fiction. 3. Relato-- Fiction. 4. Mind/Bodybuilders — Fiction.

For my two sons
    — Cricket Casey

For my mother Sarah
    — Grandmaster Melle Mel

CONTENTS

1   Movin' On 6
2   The Adventure Begins 8
3   Time Warp 11
4   Battle of the Viroids 23
5   The Magician of the Mind 43
6   Viroid Extraction 54
7   "I Want Answers!" 67
8   Flashback 71
9   Future Flash 75
10 Escape from Angroid and Graboid 90
11 Biofitness Fun 98
Inner National Bank of Worth 116
Glossary 117

SONGS

Produced by Joey Mekkah of Black Solaris Entertainment

Destiny
Performed and written by Melle Mel 18

Viroid Battle Song
Performed and written by Melle Mel 25

Get a Life
Performed and written by Melle Mel 49

Fountain of Truth
Performed and arranged by Lady Gaga
Featuring Melle Mel
Written by Melle Mel and Cricket Casey 64

When I Laugh
Performed by Melle Mel and Joey Mekkah
Written by Melle Mel 87

World Family Tree
Performed by Melle Mel/Featuring Lady Gaga
Outro by Brittany Beall 95

Activity-Not Passivity
Performed by Melle Mel
Written by Melle Mel and Cricket Casey 110

"Grandmaster Melle Mel has done it again! Melle Mel and Casey have written and produced a read 'n' rap fable with a new message for our youth through story and hip-hop songs, to help kids choose the right path of activity-not passivity. Read 'n' rap with your kids and join Melle Mel and Lady Gaga as they give a Grammy-worthy performances. It's "The Message" that counts and Melle and Casey are our kind of messengers for the future."

— QUINCY JONES

Chapter 1. Movin' On

"Ow! That's mean!" cried Joey as his older brother, Scott, changed the channel on the TV set. It was in the middle of Joey's favorite program, and Scott slapped him on the head as he did it.

"Scott! Go to your room until dinner," his mother ordered. "And I want you to read one of your books about how to be a little nicer to people." Scott's mother was losing her patience with his nasty, angry moods.

Eleven-year-old Scott and six-year-old Joey had recently moved from a large house with a yard in the suburbs to an apartment in the city with no yard at all. Now they were cramped into a small apartment with two bedrooms and a living room, which also served as the dining area, TV room, and playroom. When you fit the contents of four rooms into one room, it can be quite cluttered. You really have to downsize when

"Ahh-h-h-o-o-o-oh!"

you're living in New York City.

Scott was used to having his own bed-room complete with a computer, an XBox, and his own toys. Joey had a smaller room, but now they had to share a bedroom and everything in it. Scott was not happy with this situation. He resented having to share with Joey and had become selfish and mean. The next day, Joey was going to a birthday party and Scott was relieved that he would have a day to himself.

Chapter 2. The Adventure Begins

That morning, after taking Joey to the birthday party, Scott's mother was in the kitchen preparing lunch when Scott walked in complaining. "I'm bored. There's nothing to do in this stupid apartment. I wish we were back in our house. I hate it here!"

"This will give you something to do," his mother said as she handed him a plate. "I've made your favorite sandwich, peanut butter and jelly—with the crust removed, just the way you like it."

With Joey at the birthday party, Scott

realized he didn't know what to do with himself.

"After lunch," Mother suggested, "why don't you call those kids you met in school who live in the building, and I'll take you to Central Park. You can find plenty to do there on a beautiful day like this."

Angelina, who was in Scott's class, and Eli, who was in a class behind them, were happy to be included on the excursion. They walked along the path past the lake and the rowboats to a bench in the shade where his mother could read her magazine while the kids played.

"Hey, Mom," Scott asked, "want to play catch with us?"

"Later," Mother said. "Let me finish reading this article."

As Scott and his friends wandered down the path toward a graceful little bridge that arched over a stream, his mother called after him, "Scott, don't go too far away."

"We just want to see the bridge." They

"Where am I? Who are you?"

strolled onto the bridge, and out of curiosity Scott leaned over the railing. "Did you
see that?" he shouted.

"What?" said Eli.

"There," Angelina said, pointing. "I see
it. It's moving. Scott leaned farther out. Suddenly, he lost his balance and flipped head
over heels into the green water, howling as
he dropped, "Ah-h-h-o-o-o-oh! Help!"

Eli and Angelina could only watch helplessly as Scott fell.

Chapter 3. Time Warp

As he hit the water, everything went hazy, and Scott closed his eyes. He suddenly felt small, paw-like hands grabbing his arms and legs and dragging him deep into a stream that began to swirl like a whirlpool, sucking him down through a dark tunnel. It was really a portal into another dimension, a unique point in space and time peopled by strange creatures.

When Scott opened his eyes, he found himself in a dark room, stretched out on a table like the one he had seen in Dr. Gandy's office. His hands and feet were bound with sticky string, and strange creatures were jumping up and down around the table chattering about what they were planning to do to him.

Angroid, the big red ugly one shaped like a flame with warts, horns, pointy ears, and piercing lime-green eyes, said, "Where shall we zap the anger ray, Fearoid? In his chest or in his brain?"

Fearoid, a small purple creature with wide, frightened eyes, was holding tightly to Scott because he feared the boy might break free.

"Let me at him, Fearoid!" Angroid growled, aiming a zapper at Scott.

Scott began to panic and struggled to free himself.

Fearoid leaned over and stuttered, "H-h-here, A-a-angroid, I th-th-think his h-h-head is the b-b-best p-p-place for t-t-the a-a-anger z-z-zap."

"Get away from me!" Scott screamed.

"H-h-he's g-g-getting l-l-loose!" Fearoid yelled. "U-u-use your z-z-zapper N-N-NOW, A-A-Angroid!"

Scott was squirming and turning his

head from side to side. Angroid pushed Fearoid aside and shouted, "Get out of the way, you stuttering fool!" He proceeded to zap Scott in the chest. Scott screamed and writhed as he tugged at the ropes that bound his hands.

Angroid, smiling his wicked smile and laughing his evil laugh, rasped, "Once we get control of him, he'll be ours forever! Ha-ha-ha-ha-ha! And if we gain control of the children, we will eventually control the world! One bad apple can spoil the whole bunch. If we plant a few seeds of anger, we can get a chain reaction of anger going from kid to kid… from household to household… from school to school… from state to state… country to country… and then all the children in the world will be under our control. The media will help by spreading the worrisome word of social tensions everywhere. They are like parrots; they repeat information over and over. There will be no stopping us; soon everyone will be under our control—which means out of control! Ha-ha-ha-ha-ha!"

"W-w-what ab-b-bout the ad-d-dults?" Fearoid interjected.

Angroid shrieked furiously and shoved Fearoid, "You dimwit, just who do you think the future adults are?" He was losing his patience with Fearoid's lack of comprehension.

"A-a-all th-th-these k-k-kids?" Fearoid spit out.

"Yes, you simpleton, I don't know how I put up with you." Angroid growled, as he turned to acknowledge his name being called by a two-headed, green, spider-like creature, with four legs, four arms, and an enormous potbelly who had crept up to Scott. He was the one who had tied Scott up with the sticky string that dripped from his fingers. "Got your zapper, Graboid?" Angroid inquired.

"Sure do," chortled Graboid, "This will make him gross and greedy!" And with a sinister laugh, he zapped Scott in the belly.

As Scott shrieked again, Angroid jumped around gleefully shouting. "Yes, yes, total control! If we can control kids' emotions, we can dominate the world!"

Seeing Angroid's excitement, Fearoid became more courageous. "I c-c-can r-r-radiate a f-f-fear virus. I c-c-can z-z-zap him with f-f-fear. F-f-fear c-c-combined with a-a-anger and g-g-greed! He w-w-will s-s-spread them l-l-like the f-f-flu."

The three creatures joined hands and danced around Scott screeching and bellowing, "If we control the children, we can control the world, control the world, c-c-control the w-w-world. We can spread fear everywhere, spread fear everywhere, s-s-spread f-f-fear e-e-every wh-wh-where!"

"Get away from me!" Scott yelled, "Help! Somebody help me! PLEASE!"

Scott's anguished "PLEASE!" a magic word in any language, brought forth a flash of light. Suddenly a small, smiling, turtle-like being with a shimmering silvery shell as buoyant as a bubble appeared on Scott's shoulder. As the turtle appeared, the Viroids backed off into a corner. Scott could feel that positive energy radiating from the turtle's shining shell dissolving the negativity of the weird creatures. Viroids are loathsome creatures that love the dark and cannot stand intense brightness. It caused them to immediately scatter and disappear as quickly as you can change your mind.

"Who are you?" Scott asked in amazement.

"I'm Taki, your soulman," the turtle proclaimed in a loud, clear voice as he proceeded to set Scott free. "I'm your alter ego, your inner friend. You called for help, so here I am.

Scott was near tears with relief. "Those creatures were trying to kill me!" he wailed.

Taki ejected from his shell and, skipping around to Scott's chest, he said, "They're Viroids, which are negative emotions. They were trying to ruin your life—

not take it."

"What are emotions? I've never heard of them."

"They are that part of you that involves your feelings — happiness and sadness; love and hate; joy and sorrow."

Scott groaned, "Well, now I feel awful."

"Exactly! They were trying to control your emotions — to aggravate you and make you feel bad and mean."

"What can I do to feel better, Taki?" Scott asked in desperation."

You have an important life to live," Taki explained cheerfully as he sat on his shell and crossed his legs. Pointing his index finger at Scott, he said, "The world needs you. There is a job that only you can do, but you must conquer the Viroids, and master your emotions. Where's your courage, kid? You're not dying, kid. Quit all that crying. Are you listening? Are you hearing? Brace up, smarten up, and listen to my song." Suddenly, Taki jumped up on top of his shell and started to sing boisterously…

Destiny Song
Performed by Grandmaster Melle Mel

Be what you wanna. Do what you really wanna.
Learn what you wanna. Live where you really wanna.
Have what you want to. Give what you really wanna.
Go where you wanna. See what you really wanna.

Whenever you feel the art of the deal,
Reinvent the wheel and be relentless at whatever is real.
Nothing is signed and sealed or prearranged.
Everything is subject to change.
Anything can be rearranged.
Things readjust, can be realigned, can be calibrated,

Moved, distorted, it could be
shortened or elevated,
Manipulated, but one thing's true'
Do what you do, 'cause Destiny
means that you were meant to be
you.

Be what you wanna. Do what you
really wanna.
Learn what you wanna. Live where
you really wanna.
Have what you want to. Give what you
really wanna.
Go where you wanna. See what you
really wanna.

The power is yours, the hours and
the minutes,
And the days and the weeks, in the
peak of the tower is yours.
The truth and the light source, the
brightness,
The heights of righteous as far as it
gets, it's infinite,
It's eternity, farther than the mind

can see.
It's reality, visions even the blind can
see.
Sounds that even the deaf can hear.
Destiny, it's meant to be, please don't
have no fear!

Be what you wanna. Do what you
really wanna.
Learn what you wanna. Live where
you really wanna.
Have what you want to. Give what you
really wanna.
Go where you wanna. See what you
really wanna.

Be a tutor, teacher, preacher, pastor,
be a governor,
president, a judge, or grandmaster,
doctor, lawyer, a senator,
A general, town council, city, state, or
federal,
A lieutenant, an entrepreneur, the
inspector, a movie star, the producer,
Or the director, a songwriter, a

singer, a chef.
Destiny, whatever you do, make sure
you do it your best.

Be what you wanna. Do what you
really wanna.
Learn what you wanna. Live where
you really wanna.
Have what you want to. Give what you
really wanna.
Go where you wanna. See what you
really wanna.

With great effort, Scott tried to get up. "I'm so weak," he gasped. "Taki, I can hardly sit up."

Taki looked him over and exclaimed as he donned his shell, "Scott, this is a critical time. You'll need all your inner strength to understand and control your emotions. Don't crumble on me, boy! We have to make it to the Battle Meadow before the Viroids come back with reinforcements!"

Taki pushed a button on the front of his carapace and a tortoiseshell cell phone popped up. He flipped it open and made an urgent call uttering a secret password, "Bonabakula!" Then he said, "The Viroids are trying to take over another child! Send the Cortex Rescue Team to the Battle Meadow, immediately!"

Snapping the phone shut, he attempted to rouse the fainting boy by singing more of the "Destiny Song"…

Be what you wanna. Do what you wanna.
Learn what you wanna. Live where you really wanna.
Have what you want to. Give what you really wanna.
Go where you really wanna. See what you really wanna.

Scott felt drained of every last bit of energy. As he closed his eyes and fell into a deep sleep, an owl, whom Taki called Gam-

From a bird's eye view, Scott watches in awe as opposing forces clash.

ba, swooped down and whisked the slumbering boy away.

Chapter 4. Battle of the Viroids

Gamba deposited Scott in a huge nest high up in a tree overlooking the Battle Meadow. Its trunk was the size of a small house, with branches the width of a room. The nest was constructed of flexible twigs lined with soft moss. The owl looked over Scott like a mother bird guarding her young.

As Scott slept, Taki hovered above the nest like a flying saucer, then zoomed off outstripping the wind, and landed in the meadow in time to greet the Cortex Rescue Team of Mind/Bodybuilders approaching from the south. The grass spread across this vast field like a lush green velvet carpet. There were beautiful, colorful flowers and bushes along the southern border wafting a strong sweet fragrance across the field. On the northern ridge, however, was a dark forest of sinister-looking trees where the unknown lurked.

Suddenly, loud sirens blared and a host of Viroids swarmed out of the perimeter of the woods. Taki materialized at Scott's side just as he awakened. Together they peered out of the nest and gazed upon the ghastly creatures, shooting their lasers and zappers everywhere, screaming and screeching their horrible battle song ...

Viroid Battle Song
Performed by Grandmaster Melle Mel

In your mind we are strong, and we
are wrong,
And this is our Battle Song.
We make you want to fight and fuss,
And we're so mean that we're even
scared of us.
In your mind we are strong, and we
are wrong,
And this is our Battle Song.
We make you want to fight and fuss,
And we're so mean that we're even
scared of us.
We made you angry, we made you
scream,
Late at night we made you have bad
dreams.
We play tricks with your head.
In the morning, we get you up on the
wrong side of the bed.

We make you wanna disrespect,
Fill your mind with strife, until your
whole life is a wreck,
Even then you won't have a clue,
'Cause what we do, is take total
control of you.

In your mind we are strong, and we
are wrong,
And this is our Battle Song.
We make you want to fight and fuss,
And we're so mean that we're even
scared of us.

We invade your brain with fear and
paranoia.
Hit you with a soul destroyer.
Shoot you with the angry laser,
And when we daze ya,
We'll zap you with the mind eraser.
Blow after blow we'll slow your
motion,
Till you can't feel your feelings or
control your emotions.
To us, fear is great,

And we won't stop until the only thing
you know is hate!

In your mind we are strong, and we
are wrong,
And this is our Battle Song.
We make you want to fight and fuss,
And we're so mean that we're even
scared of us.

United we stand. With our hands we
poke and punch,
Keep in mind; we eat humankind for
lunch,
Keep in mind; we're psychopathic and
deranged,
And do everything to make you act
strange.
Make you wanna act a fool.
We make you wanna get up, and
never come back to school.
We make you wanna waste your day.
You waste so many days that you
throw your whole life away.

In your mind we are strong, and we
are wrong.
And this is our Battle Song.
We make you want to fight and fuss,
And we're so mean that we're even
scared of us.

We are the Viroids; we will release a
virus of emotion.
We have Angroids, Graboids, and
Fearoids.
We are calling them to harm.
The Viroids will rule.
The Viroids will crush.
Ultimately the Viroids will destroy.

From their bird's—eye view in the tree,
Scott and Taki watched in awe as the opposing forces clashed amid clouds of smoke,
with shrieks and howls and the crash of
weaponry. The Cortex Mind/Bodybuilders
challenged the grotesque army of Viroids,
including Angroid, Fearoid, Graboid, Vain-
oid, Lazyoid, Bullyoid, Boredoid, Snoboid,

Wimpoid, Tearoid, Craboid and Paranoid.

With shields clanging, and zappers zapping, dozens of giant Mind/Bodybuilders were led onto the field by four powerful beings bearing freeze guns and laser beams for weaponry—Mikala, Zocko, Sitara, and Tia. The Mind/Bodybuilders were the martial guards of Cortex. Every member of the Cortex team was proportionally trim and muscular; all were highly educated in mind, body and spirit.

Scott wondered who these Mind/Bodybuilders were. He knew the Viroids were the negative evil tempters. Taki explained that the Mind/Bodybuilders represented the positive forces for good in his life.

Zocko, the brawny, wheelchair-bound Mind/Bodybuilder with four sinewy arms and spiked blond hair, immobilized the trembling Fearoid with a freeze gun, stopping him cold. Zocko's corps, each with four muscular arms swinging freeze guns, turned the Viroids into motionless statues. Scott could see the angry and bitter expressions on their frozen faces. Other Cortex Mind/ Bodybuilders used laser beams in battle that shocked the enemies into paralysis.

"Why is Zocko in a wheelchair?" Scott asked.

"Zocko injured his spinal cord in an accident leaving him paralyzed from the waist down," explained Taki. "His arms are strong and he sure can move in that chair," Scott noted. "That's just it! He's completely functional because he makes the most out of what he has."

Scott had to agree. He was seeing Zocko in battle using two arms for freeze guns and two arms to spin his turbo-blaster wheelchair around on a dime.

Mikala, a husky, bronze warrior with a shaved head, sporting diamond-stud earrings and a weight belt, was the leader of the Positive Force in the brigade. He was expertly melting Viroids and their legion of demons with his ray gun.

Sitara, the elegantly plumed Queen of Self-Esteem, zoomed gracefully down on the Viroids, defeating them with her magical golden water ring. Angroid dashed madly toward her with his zapper aimed to strike.

Soaring up over him, she pinched her water ring ejecting a stream of rainbow water which dissolved the rays of the zapper instantly, and swirled Angroid into a puddle on the ground. All around, the forces clashed, and gradually the Viroids were driven from the Battle Meadow.

Beautiful Tia, tawny and muscular, the powerful Princess of Tough Love, dressed in a toga with a glowing heart emblem buckling her belt, flew onto the Battle Meadow riding Zamir, her multicolored parrot, as the fighting subsided. Shooting barrages of love arrows with heart tips, she imbued those remaining with love.

As the smoke cleared and the sun began to shine brightly on the picturesque, peaceful, green meadow, Taki turned to Scott and said, "I'll always be here when you need me," then disappeared in a flash of light.

In the distance the Cortex Team was performing body-shaping movements in synchronized patterns. Watching them, Scott understood why the Mind/Body-builders were in such excellent physical condition, and so mentally sharp in comparison to the nervous, miserable, twitching Viroids.

He jumped as he felt a tap on his shoulder. "Hi Scott, I'm Tia. That was a hard-fought victory," Tia commented as she surveyed the scene.

"What type of workout are they doing over there, Tia?" Scott inquired, holding up his arm to check his muscles. He wanted to develop muscles like theirs.

"Oh, they are performing the biofitness shapes. They are fun to do once you master them. Zocko and his group are doing push-ups. Mikala is leading his group through the bird-dog position, the cat stretch, the bow, the swimmer, and the stomach crunch. They strengthen, stretch, and relax you at the same time. We like to work from the core out."

Scott looked puzzled. "What's the core?"

"Core muscles are the muscles that keep your body centered. They are important for posture, coordination, and balance," Tia explained.

"Wow, I like the names of those exercises," Scott exclaimed as he lay down on his back and proceeded to do a stomach crunch. He was thrilled when he discovered that he could feel his core. "I wish my school had a class in biofitness! Maybe then all the kids wouldn't be so obsessed and negative about their appearance."

"Schools here in Cortex are set up totally different from those on Earth. Your schools concentrate mainly on intellectual energy, measuring your intelligence quotient, or IQ. We train both mind and body from the beginning. We start our children at a very young age at the Biorhythm Academy."

"What is a biorhythm?" asked Scott in wonderment.

"A biorhythm is composed of the three cycles of energy levels we all experience daily. Everyone possesses physical energy, emotional or spiritual energy, and intellectual energy. We measure all — physical quotient, PQ; emotional quotient, EQ; as well as intelligence quotient, IQ.

"Our goal on Cortex is to maintain our biorhythms at an optimal level to keep all three energy levels in harmony. Earthlings tend to direct almost all of their education in schools to the intellectual cycle, ignoring the emotional and the physical. This throws off your biorhythms leaving you wide open for stress. Viroids love to attack tired, out-of-shape bodies and flagging spirits."

"My school is boring," Scott griped. "We have gym twice a week and music and art only once a week." The rest of the time we have to sit and listen to long, dull lessons, and we aren't allowed to get out of our seats. They must not know about biorhythms."

"Humans tend to have a very lopsided spirit," Tia responded with sympathy as she shook her head.

"Music is an extremely important vibratory energy source needed in any culture to holistically connect all the kinetic forces and provide an intellectual and stress-free society. You see Scott, by combining language, which is left brained, with music, which is right brained, you become in tune with yourself and your environment.

"For example, people sing and animals howl, while trees and plants sway and dance to the wind's whistle. Like a fine instrument, we like to keep in tune and harmony with ourselves and nature. I think you know what can happen if we are out of tune."

Scott jumped in with unexpected confidence, "Oh yeah, like an out-of-tune instrument producing bad sounds and bad vibrations — like thunder, earthquakes, hurricanes, and the Viroid's Battle song. That was really eerie."

"You catch on quickly, Scott," Tia praised. "Here on Cortex we combine speaking and singing to communicate. As the famous poet Percy Bysshe Shelley once wrote, 'Music, when soft voices die, vibrates in the memory.'"

Scott blurted out, "Oh, is that why sometimes I hear a song and I can't get it out of my head?"

Tia laughed, "Yes, I think that happens to all of us."

"Boy, that would be awesome if I went to school and we sang conversations with all my friends and teachers," Scott chuckled gleefully. "Singing makes me feel good."

Tia smiled knowingly. "The subjects of mathe-matics, science, english and history are all very important to learn, but your life will be unbalanced and difficult if you ignore your emotional and physical training, EQ and PQ. Tell me what exercise is, Scott."

Scott shrugged his shoulders. "Isn't it when you go to the gym and lift weights and work on those funny-looking machines? They'd never put them in my school," he added discouragingly.

"That is only a small part of it," Tia explained. "For example, did you know that exercise is different in every culture? When we study history, we could spend months just on the history of the development of exercise and physical fitness."

Scott looked surprised. "I never thought of exercise as a part of history."

"The art of exercise has many forms. We have the Japanese and Chinese martial arts; yoga from India; Pilates originating in

Germany; and tribal dance forms from both American Indians and from Africa—many focusing on discipline and balance. This all has to do with your biorhythms and also New Physics. Exercise should be fun, and the right attitude and training are important as for any task."

"What is New Physics?" Scott inquired eagerly as he executed a bear stance biofitness position, mimicking the Mind/Bodybuilders.

"It's the study of all of life's forces, energies, and vibrations," Tia explained, "but you will hear about that later."

"I feel like I don't know anything," Scott sighed. "I wish I could go to the Biorhythm Academy."

Tia leaned over and whispered into Scott's ear. "Maybe I can work something out with Relato."

"Who?" Scott asked, perplexed.

"Relato, the Master of Reality, the Magnificent Magician of the Mind. Listen, we have a lot to do," she interjected as Sitara flew over, leaving the Mind/Bodybuilders in the distance to continue their routine. "You will meet him later; now I want you to meet Sitara. She is an important member of our team."

"How are you doing, Scott?" Sitara asked as she put her arm around his shoulder comfortingly.

"I'm feeling better," he told her, rubbing his forehead. It was all very strange. His body felt exhausted from this ordeal, yet his mind was running in overdrive attempting to absorb all these new ideas and experiences.

"Hop on, Scott!" Tia invited. Her parrot, Zamir, equipped with bucket seats like an airplane, had alighted and was awaiting her orders.

Scott's eyes widened with surprise! This was the biggest bird with the brightest colors that he had ever seen, and he had certainly never ridden on a giant parrot before!

Enthralled, he climbed aboard and asked, "Where are we going?"

"We're going to see Relato," Tia explained, as they took off with a flap of the parrot's wings. They were carried through the air, gliding up and down like the most magnificent noiseless roller coaster soaring over, under, and around clouds that looked like pink cotton candy in the back-glow of the setting sun.

This is a long day, thought Scott, as he looked back at the fading green meadow.

"Look ahead, my friend," Tia urged as she pointed to the building with a tall geyser-like fountain and wonderful dancing waters.

"Hey, Tia, I see a rainbow!" Scott whooped excitedly.

The distant images became larger as they approached. When the parrot landed, Scott was mesmerized. They were in front of a beautiful fountain of artistically carved stone. Myriad streams of multicolored water were shooting high into the air, forming infinite rainbows.

It was the most fantastic fountain display Scott had ever seen. The word "VERITAS" was carved into the rim of the fountain. Behind the fountain was an enormous building with huge pillars.

Stone figures graced the triangular pediment above the grand entry, and chiseled over the doors were the words, "Inner National Bank of Worth." It looked like a Grecian temple.

Scott pointed at the fountain in wonder and asked, "What is that?"

"That, Scott," Tia responded with pride, "is the Fountain of Truth. The waters are magical and rich in minerals. The rainbow spray exudes a positive energy that is healing and relaxing. We drink from it, bathe in it, splash in it, play in it, swim in it, sing in it, and most of all, learn from it."

She escorted him up the many steps leading to the gigantic building.

The Inner National Bank of Worth and the
Fountain of Truth

"Is this where Relato, the Master of
Reality, the Magnificent Magician of the
Mind lives?" Scott asked, thinking to him-
self, whatever that means!

"No, he lives in the castle beyond," Tia smiled. "You will be in good hands. Now, I must go to teach at the Academy. I'll catch up with you later."

As Scott approached, the immense doors swung open.

Chapter 5. The Magician of the Mind

Hesitantly, Scott walked into a wide, elegant foyer with murals painted on the walls depicting the Mind/Bodybuilders in their various activities. A crystal chandelier with at least fifty sparkling lights illuminated the hall.

A tall, handsome man with shiny straight white hair, dressed in rich, colorful robes was walking toward him. The room reminded Scott of a castle he had seen in a movie. In one hand, the man held a scepter glowing with a radiating light that was more like a luminous energy source.

When he smiled, his white teeth gleamed against his coppertoned skin and lit up his perceptive sea-green eyes. He was a giant; but his aura was gentle, and Scott wasn't frightened.

"Where am I?" Scott inquired.

The man smiled and spoke in a deep vibrant voice that enveloped Scott with calm. "You are in Cortex, the Inner Dimension."

Scott looked puzzled.

"I am Relato, the Lord of Cortex, Master of Reality, Magician of the Mind. This is the throne room in the Hall of Truth and Beauty. I appear along the Path."

Scott looked in all directions. "I don't see a path." Indeed, this place was not like a path at all. I'm here, Scott thought, but "here" seemed like nowhere he had ever known before.

Relato read Scott's mind and without moving his lips said, *Can you hear my voice?*

"Yes," Scott said, surprised that he was having a conversation, but he was the only one talking.

But *I'm not speaking*, declared the man.

"Then how do I know what you are saying?"

Scott was dumbfounded and rubbed his eyes to make sure that he was really not seeing Relato's lips move. He was amazed to realize that Relato was transferring thoughts without speaking.

Relato stroked his chin, watching Scott trying to figure out what was happening. Then he raised his finger and said out loud, "When you're alone in your room and you think of a bicycle, what do you see in your mind?"

"A bicycle," Scott blurted out. His eyes grew wider with excitement because he surmised the answer.

"But is it there?"

"No, but I see it in my thoughts."

"Aha! In your thoughts! And can you imagine peddling down the road, so you have the pleasure of riding it even though it isn't there?"

"I guess so," Scott admitted, scratching his head and marveling at that thought.

"Here in Cortex, what we think can be heard; what we imagine can be seen and touched. You are in the place of beginnings and endings, of comings and goings."

"How did I get here?"

"You were on the Path."

"But, I don't remember seeing a path." Scott looked around again in bewilderment.

"It's not something you can see, that's why."

"Then how can I be on it?" Scott retorted with a noticeable inflection of frustration emerging in his voice.

Relato spread his arms with a confident grin and asked, "Don't you know what the Path is?" Relato seemed to hold many secrets but would tell none of them. Scott realized he would have to figure things out for himself.

"Let me ask you something." Relato leaned down placing one hand on Scott's shoulder and looking him in the eye. "Why do you get angry at your mother?"

Scott was surprised that Relato knew this about him. "She's always saying, 'watch out,' 'be careful,' 'don't go there,' 'don't do that,' 'stay away from this,' 'get away from that.' She makes me feel like a baby."

Tia had returned and was suddenly present beside them, as though she had appeared from thin air. She smiled and said, "May I tell him, Relato?"

Relato nodded, and Tia put her hand gently on Scott's arm. "Fearoid had you in his power. He sucked your strength by turning your fear into anger, and anger was ruining your ability to make sensible decisions."

"Mom is always too busy to play with

me," Scott tried to explain. "She says, 'not now' or 'later,' and 'later' never comes!"

Relato smiled. "Oh, I see, so it's your mother's fault?"

"I'm sick and tired of being told what to do," Scott ranted and stamped his foot. "I don't have to listen to anybody. I'm tired of being ordered around. I hate all adults!"

Relato laughed, "Listen to that, Tia! My, oh my, listen to all that negativity! Somebody has to be de-Viroided! What do you think, Taki?"

Taki had materialized on Scott's shoulder and had quickly pulled his head into his shell at Scott's outburst.

Now he poked it out again and admonished Scott. "Pick up little fellow, why so green and yellow? Have you been infected? Are you feeling dejected? Got anger inside; self-pity besides? Get a life, man. End all that strife, man," and Taki began to merrily sing...

Get a Life
Performed by Grandmaster Melle Mel

Life - do the right thing, have a nice
day.
Life - not the wrong way, do it the
right way.
Life - have a good time, come on and
celebrate.
Life - no need to hesitate before you
graduate.
Life - get a good job and a nice house.
Life - and a nice car and a nice
spouse.
Life - you have it in you, now bring it
out of you.
Life - keep it positive, and make me
proud of you.

Keep your eyes on your prize, and
follow your dreams.
The road is long, but it ain-t as hard
as it seems,
And find yourself a guiding light.
Stay strong and everything will be

alright.
Live right, work hard for the money you earn.
Learn to teach and to strive, to teach and learn.
Live in peace free from strife,
And before you do anything, you gotta GET A LIFE!
Do the right thing, have a nice day.
Life - not the wrong way, do it the right way.
Life - have a good time, come on and celebrate.
Life - no need to hesitate before you graduate.
Life - get a good job and a nice house.
Life - and a nice car and a nice spouse.
Life - you have it in you, now bring it out of you.
Life - keep it positive, and make me proud of you.

Some kids go to school to steal and lie,

Thinkin' that high school is a place to get high.
Playin' hooky and stayin' at home,
Thinkin' they all grown while they're runnin' up a bill on the phone.
Actin' fresh and talkin' loud,
Smokin' weed, stayin' out, now they're hangin' with the wrong crowd,
Walkin' 'round with a gun and a knife.
I think before you go and get shot, you better GET A LIFE!

Do the right thing. Have a nice day.
Life - not the wrong way, do it the right way.
Life - have a good time, come on and celebrate.
Life - no need to hesitate before you graduate.
Life - get a good job, and a nice house.
Life - and a nice car, and a nice spouse.
Life - you have it in you, now bring it out of you.

Life - keep it positive, and make me proud of you.

You can still learn while doing your thing.
Get a degree, get rap, and play, or sing.
Write your rhymes, explore your art.
See you can get a PhD and still be street smart.
You could be the head of the class; you got it made,
And you could be the one to find a cure for AIDS,
Within you is all the answers.
See, you could be a dancer and still find the cure for cancer.

Life - do the right thing, have a nice day.
Life - not the wrong way, do it the right way.
Life - have a good time, come on and celebrate.
Life - no need to hesitate before you

"Find yourself a guiding light. Stay strong and every thing will be alright."

graduate.
Life - get a good job, and a nice house.
Life - and a nice car, and a nice spouse.
Life - you have it in you, now bring it out of you.
Life - keep it positive and make me proud of you.

GET A LIFE!

☆ ☆ ☆

Chapter 6. Viroid Extraction

Relato called Mikala and Sitara to come and take Scott to the Viroid extraction chamber. "He needs a thorough Attitude Reversal and Emotional Immunity Enhancement Program."

"Wait a minute! Where are you taking me? Taki! Help! Help me! PLEASE! I don't want to go anywhere!" Scott cried. "No more adventures! PLEASE! I'm sorry. I'm … so sorreeee …"

At that entreaty, Taki swirled in his silvery shell. Smiling, he said in a soothing voice, "Don't worry, Scott. We are all here to help you, but you have to get rid of your fear and hostility. This is for your own good and I promise you'll feel better afterwards. You will learn from the Mind/Body Team how to build your energy shields against the Viroids."

Mikala, leader of Positive Force in the battle brigade, and Sitara, Queen of Self-

Esteem, led Scott into a room that had all four walls and ceiling painted a pale blue like the sky. It contained a small garden of plants with a waterfall and stream cultivating its own ecosystem. Four reclining chairs resembling spaceship bucket seats floated in midair defying gravity. Scott was carefully settled into one, and soon, as he was surrounded by faint music, soft lights, and changing colors, he slowly relaxed and closed his eyes.

He could hear a fading conversation between Relato and Taki, who had followed. Relato waved his scepter over Scott's head and a warm blanket of luminous light encompassed his body.

"It's a tough job watching over all the children, Taki," Relato declared with a confident smile. "Youngsters must be taught to use their cortexes instead of their reflexes. They must be active instead of reactive. They must be taught to realize that their lives are up to them, and that their choices become deposits or withdrawals in their Inner National Bank of Worth."

"Exactly!" said Taki, who was perched on Relato's forearm like a falcon. "I'm teaching all who will listen," he assured Relato, "but they must give consent! That means they are ready to learn. Grownups call it an open mind. With Scott, all I can do is stick to his shoulder and be there for him when he needs my help."

The words of "Destiny Song" swirled like visions in Scott's heart and mind, and when he finally opened his eyes Relato was smiling at him. "Better now?"

"Yes," Scott said, "I think so. But why won't the Viroids leave me alone?"

"Viroids are horrid creatures. Erupting emotions from within, they corrupt everyone. Not just you; even your mother and father."

Scott started to jump up from the chair shouting in disbelief, "Not my mother and father!"

"Relax," said Relato placing his hand on Scott's shoulder urging him to sit back. "It is like getting a flu or a cold in your thoughts and feelings instead of your body. They saturate your energy field with negativity and throw you out of control. Feelings are easily spread to other people. They generate reactions of anger, self-pity, jealousy, greed, boredom, and hatred. It becomes difficult to think. But they can't take over unless you let them."

"But I don't want them," Scott insisted.

"Then you must think more of others," Relato expounded. He looked at Taki who nodded in agreement. "That will build up your immunity. Viroids attack when all you think of is yourself. As I said, you are on a Path."

"What path?" Scott was beginning to feel annoyed and frustrated again. "I still don't get what you mean. I can't see any path."

"The Path is your experience and is

always behind you, that's why you can't see it." Relato gestured with a turn of his head. "Its stepping stones are the choices you have made in the past. You can choose the path of honesty, kindness, and love, or the path of deceit, anger, greed, and cruelty. The world you leave behind will impel you toward your future. Making the right choices on your Path in life is the key."

"Can't I just take a pill or something, like when I get sick?" Scott replied, throwing out his palms in dismay.

"Maybe for a cold infection, but not for an emotional infection such as anger or greed. There are, however, tools that will help. Did you notice how Zocko used his shield on the battlefield? Let me have Zocko explain."

Relato waved his scepter and Zocko in his turbo-blaster wheelchair instantly materialized from the back garden area.

"Scott wants to know about your shield." Relato patted Zocko on his shoulder as Zocko steered confidently over to Scott.

"Proud to be asked to help the lad," Zocko said, "A shield is based on the importance of prevention. It's like immunization. Sometimes it's too late if anger and fear have penetrated your energy field. There is an invisible energy field around everyone. It's called an aura, and it's chock full of all our ideas, opinions, and feelings, both positive and negative. If Angroid zaps into your field with anger, all the colors and vibrations of the field change. The shield can hold off those attacks if we build it up good and strong."

Scott was growing more interested, "What is immunization? Can I build a strong shield like yours?"

"Of course you can. Immunization is a resistance. If you are immune to something, it will not affect you." Zocko held up his shield in front of him.

"Remember the importance of your choices. The shield is made of honesty and kindness, as Relato said. Each time you control your temper, the shield gets stronger, tougher, and more resistant to attack from Viroids, or anyone else for that matter.

Everyone gets angry, sad, jealous, greedy, or hateful at times. For example, your brother, your friends, and sometimes even your parents have those feelings. We all need mental fitness training as well as bodily fitness training."

"Do I have an energy field?" Scott inquired as he copied Zocko's martial arts moves with an imaginary shield.

"Everyone has an energy field. We call this study the New Physics."

Scott's face lit up. He remembered that Tia had mentioned New Physics. "What is that?"

"First off," Zocko answered, pleased to be able to show off his knowledge, "Physics is the science that studies matter and energy, and the interactions between the two. This includes the study of gravity, magnetic forces, electricity, and heat, as well as atoms and nuclear energy."

Scott was impressed. "Wow! That sounds complicated!"

"Our New Physics studies the emotions, and positive and negative forces. We have discovered that some people have strong energy fields while other people have weak energy fields. We are learning how to make weak fields stronger. Don't forget, it's up to us to build up our bodies and our minds."

"What does that have to do with your shield?" Scott interjected as he gestured with his imaginary shield.

"The shield is for psychological immunity."

"What's that?"

"Psychological immunity is when you are able to build up a resistance to emotional outbursts such as anger, fear, greed, and hatred. The shield holds off negative reactions." Zocko spun his wheelchair around, holding his shield in a defensive position as if to ward off an attack.

"If, for example, you have been insulted, hurt, cheated, or bullied in school, the shield gives you a chance to stop and think. Time to stop—think—and make a choice, instead of just reacting." He raised his hand as if he were a school guard directing traffic.

"Let's say your brother breaks one of your toys, or calls you a bad name. But, instead of getting mad, you stop and think. Why did he do that? Is he mad at me? Does he want attention? Why did he call me that name? Maybe he is just reaching out for a friend in the only way he knows how."

Scott grimaced. "Breaking toys, punching, and calling names doesn't seem like a good way to make a friend."

"If you understand what's behind a person's actions, you'll have a better idea of how to handle the situation. Try it next time with your little brother, Joey, and the kids at school. Put yourself in their shoes,"

Zocko said kindly.

"Ask yourself, 'Would that action hurt me?' If the answer is yes then you know it will hurt them. When you understand a person's feelings, your emotions change and Angroid is pushed far out of your energy field, and you can take the Path of kindness. You can usually turn another's nastiness away with humor, sympathy, or a friendly comment—you never know!" Zocko winked.

It sounded logical to Scott, but he had another question. "How am I supposed to find a path I can't see because I've already walked on it?"

"The Path is your life, Scott. When you become aware of other people and your environment, you will have learned from the Path of experience and you will know truth, happiness, and fun."

Sitara and Mikala who had been standing near the doorway, and Tia, who had approached by way of the back garden, gathered around Scott, and broke into a song as they gazed out the window toward the magical fountain …

Fountain of Truth
Performed by Lady Gaga
Featuring Grandmaster Melle Mel

Everybody just clap your hands.
All the children just clap your hands
and have a ball, y'all.
(Repeat 3 times.)
I've always been looking, been trying,
been yearning,
Continually seeking, and searching
and burning,
Exploring and hunting and
everywhere turning,
For that powerful fountain, that
fountain of truth.

No answers at all, in the streets or
the mall!
I sought in the ocean; found raging
emotion.

Nothing was stable; I'm really not able
To find that powerful fountain, that
fountain of truth.

The future is yours; the time is now.
The place is near, shout loud, so
every ear can hear,
So every woman and man in the land
can understand
The new world inherited by the
children,
Free from famine and war, disease
and strife.
Free from the gun and the knife,
forever for life.
Free from all the mistakes that we
made in the past.
Throw your hands in the air and let
the truth last.

I've always been looking, been trying,
been yearning,
Continually seeking, and searching,
and burning,
Exploring, and hunting, and

everywhere turning,
For that powerful fountain, that
fountain of truth.

No answers at all, in the streets or
the mall!
I sought in the ocean; found raging
emotion.
Nothing is stable; I'm really not able
To find that powerful fountain, that
fountain of truth.

You have the power to win in every
hour,
To blossom like a flower up under a
rain shower,
To reach like the branch of the trees
in the sky.
So reach high and soar with the
eagles as we fly.
Flights with great heights, and fight
the great fights,
Strong to sing songs of wrongs that's
made right.
In the never ending search for the

fountain of truth.
In your youth you're bound to find the
fountain of truth.

I've looked in the city, a place without
pity.
Seen mountains of wealth; no
fountains of health.
Nothing is stable; I'm really not able,
To find that powerful fountain, that
fountain of truth.

Everybody just clap your hands.
All the children just clap your hands
and have a ball, y'all.
(Repeat 3 times.)
Fountain of Truth (Repeat 3 times.)

Chapter 7. "I Want Answers!"

Scott, reclining in the gravity-defying chair, was very relaxed in the Viroid extraction room with Relalto and the Mind/

"You have the power to win in every hour."

Bodybuilders. He pushed a button and the chair moved to the upright position. All of a sudden, he felt completely overwhelmed by all that had happened to him and lamented, "I have so many questions that I want answers to!"

Relato smiled patiently. "The answers you want are inside of you. By making good choices you design your own destiny. I'm not saying this is easy. The right choices are often the hardest to make. But if you can make them, you will have control over your life, and you'll realize what responsibility is all about. You will no longer blame your brother, your teachers, your friends, or your mother. You have been angry with your mother because she has had to make the choices you have been too weak and frightened to make. Viroids zapped you with fear, greed, and anger, remember? Love and kindness make us feel happy and good-natured, and people want to be around us. Fear, anger, and greed make us unhappy and hateful, and isolate us."

Scott still looked bewildered, so Relato explained it in another way. "You see, Scott, you allowed Angroid into your energy field. What we throw at others bounces back at us! Which will it be, Scott, rage or joy?"

Scott wasn't convinced. "I just want to have fun," he whined, "and I want those Viroids to leave me alone."

"Fun is what most people want." Relato grinned. "Let me ask you something. Can

"If you burst, you're only making things worse."

angry people enjoy anything? Can they enjoy eating, or playing? Do they share? Are they fun to be with? Isn't no the answer to all of these questions? Think about it, Scott, when we are overcome by anger, we are out of control. Anger and resentment lower our defense systems and leave us wide open to Viroid attacks. We burst out with words we wish we had never said and we do things that we later regret."

"I guess you're right about that," Scott said begrudgingly. "Sometimes when I get mad at Joey, I lose it—I hit him and say horrible things that I don't mean. Then I feel worse."

Relato nodded in agreement saying, "That's when you need your shield." He extended his hand and motioned for Scott to follow him.

Chapter 8. Flashback

Relato led Scott to a room that was a huge theater-in-the-round with plush, red, comfortable-looking seats.

"Wow!" said Scott, awe–stricken.

Relato, noticing that Scott's mood had changed, and that he was feeling remorse-ful and open to suggestions, said, "I have something I want to show you that may help answer some of your questions."

"Really!" Scott said eagerly.

"Cause and effect, Scott," Relato ex-pounded as he walked to the center of the stage. "Often, people don't think. They react automatically and end up regretting their actions later. Would you like to see a little replay of your past?"

"Yeah, I guess so." Scott scurried into a front row seat wondering what was going to happen next in this place of surprises.

Relato raised his scepter, and suddenly a gigantic television screen appeared in front of them like a huge hologram. Scott saw himself sitting at the family computer in the living room with Joey sitting next to him watching enviously. Joey wanted to use the computer, but Scott roughly pushed him away. A fight ensued and they fell to the floor hitting and yelling. Their mother rushed in and sent them to their room to cool off. In the end, no one got to use the computer.

Relato looked quizzically at Scott and asked, "Can you explain what just happened?"

"Joey started it! He drives me crazy!" Scott yelled defensively.

Relato held up his hand. "Stop right there. Do you see that you had a choice? You could stay crazy or you could have handled it differently. You can stop your anger at any time. That's what self-control is all about."

Scott was not convinced. "It's not that easy. Sometimes anger just takes over—the feeling is too strong!"

Relato comforted Scott by placing his arm around the boy's shoulder. "Emotions may seem overpowering at times, but you must learn to convert your anger into friendliness, which is the exact opposite. Let's say you are walking barefoot and you come upon broken glass. Would you continue walking?"

"Hmmm, of course not!" Scott was beginning to understand. "I would stop, think about it, then take a step back and walk around it."

"Exactly!" Relato exclaimed. "You can take all this dynamic energy and put it to

"No more stink'n think'n." Cooperate and you can operate

work for you instead of against you. Okay, we have seen a bit of your past; shall we look into your future?"

Scott's eyes widened with curiosity as he eagerly leaned forward to see what the big screen would show him next.

Chapter 9. Future Flash

The holographic screen flickers off and back on again. The scene is the same, except that the two brothers are sitting at the computer together. This time when Joey wants a turn with the mouse, Scott invites him to sit in his chair, and he thinks of an easy computer game they can play together.

"Want to try this?" Scott says as he leans over and shows Joey the new game. Joey is surprised and happily agrees. Scott tells him to move over so he can show him how to play the game.

Clearly, Scott is in control of his feelings and the situation has changed. They are having fun, and Joey is thrilled that Scott is taking the time to play with him.

Scott is impressed by this look into the future. "That's amazing! How did it happen?"

Relato, chuckling at Scott's reaction, indicates the screen and says, "A great playwright named Eugene O'Neill once said, 'The past is the present and the future too.' What you do determines who you are and what will happen. When you call up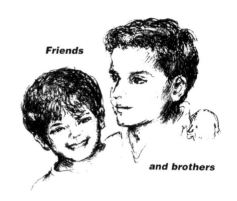

Friends

and brothers

friendliness instead of selfishness and share your knowledge with Joey that is what can happen. You make Joey happy with your generous offer to teach him the new game. This is called cooperation." He smiles with approval when he sees understanding in Scott's expression.

"You don't push him away or shut him out. You use self-control and friendliness. Emotions, like viruses, tend to replicate themselves. Everyone knows anger is contagious, but did you know that happiness is contagious, too? Which feeling would you rather catch? Which feeling would you like to spread? Rage or happiness? The choice is yours, Scott." With a wave of his scepter the holographic TV vanished.

Scott smiled up at Relato, thrilled that he was finally grasping the concept. "What you are saying is that we both feel better, and we stay friends and have fun instead of being enemies," he said excitedly. "When I'm in control of myself and manage the situation, anger doesn't explode into rage."

Relato was pleased. "Precisely! We're all in this game together, the game of life, and we need each other to make it work smoothly."

"I'm all for having fun," Scott said eagerly, "but about the Viroids — is there any way I can protect myself from them?"

"Certainly!" exclaimed Relato as he took Scott's hand. "When you arrived here did you notice the beautiful fountain? And did you read the inscription on this building?"

"Yes," said Scott, as he was guided by Relato, "I did see the fountain with the word 'VERTAS' carved in front, and water all the colors of the rainbow spraying high into the air! And I saw the words 'Inner National Bank of Worth' carved into the stone over the doors of this building. But what does it all mean, Relato?"

"That fountain is The Fountain of Truth. 'Veritas' means truth in Latin. The multicolored magical waters radiate positive energy. This building is my domain. Come with me."

They walked down a long corridor and into an enormous room that looked like a bank. Many of the inhabitants of Cortex were standing in lines leading up to windows. At each window was a penguin-like creature, resplendent in top hat and bow tie, busily tallying up deposit and withdrawal slips. The floor was covered with iridescent confetti, reminiscent of the stock exchange.

Scott was astonished and confused. "What is happening in this lively place?"

"This is our Inner National Bank where your True Net Worth is determined." Relato gestured for Scott to precede him to a table where he picked up a slip of paper called a "True Net Worth Transaction Sheet."

"How do I calculate my True Net Worth?" Scott puzzled.

"It is very simple," Relato explained in a slow, deliberate manner to make sure Scott understood. "For every positive action you set in motion, or motivate, you mark a plus one cent deposit in your account, and for every negative reaction you spark, you mark a minus one chip withdrawal."

Scott was very interested and said, "How do I keep track of these deposits and withdrawals?"

"You need to keep a journal of your cents and chips daily," Relato explained. "As your money — cents — grows, you grow in maturity — sense. They get totaled at the bank to provide you with your True Net Worth in your Growth Fund. That's what the tellers are doing so briskly behind the counters."

"Amazing! How can I start?" Scott inquired earnestly.

"You simply take this to the window, and the teller will show you how to complete it," Relato explained as he handed him a transaction sheet.

Scott went up to a window and filled the slip out for that day, checking his positive deposits and negative withdrawals. He came up a little short (more chips than cents), because he had more negatives than positives for the day, and said, "I think I need more work on my deposits," as he put some sheets in his pocket to work on later.

"You can make a list of those reactions giving you the most trouble and be ready to neutralize them. If you are aware of them you have already canceled most of their power," Relato assured him with a pat on the back. "In the battle you saw, Viroids were not eliminated, they were only stopped. You cannot eradicate them forever but you can prevent them from affecting your life! Then you can teach Joey how to do it."

"Really?" Scott smiled and wrote a plus one share on the slip, "Teaching is positive, and then he wouldn't bug me so much."

"Precisely!" Relato nodded in agreement. "Which Viroid would you like to eliminate the most?"

"Angroid is my worst enemy. He hurt me the most," Scott said with conviction.

"Angroid likes to spoil pleasure," Relato agreed, "and he ruins many friendships. What would you say is the opposite of anger?"

Scott smiled and blurted out, "Isn't it friendliness?"

"Absolutely!" replied Relato appreciatively, giving Scott two thumbs up. "Joey looks up to you as his older brother. He is eager for your friendship. You're his role model. He can learn this self-control trick from you. Just think—what is the opposite of fear?"

"Isn't it courage?" Scott declared, proud of his knowledge.

"Yes," Relato agreed. "Some folks are

afraid of the dark, and need a little light in the bedroom at night. They must say, 'I am not afraid of the dark; the dark can't hurt anyone.' Or another example would be, 'I am not afraid of thunder; the noise can't hurt anyone.' This is how we change our behavior. We substitute good for bad. Fear is an imaginary evil. As a great American president, Franklin Delano Roosevelt, once said, 'The only thing we have to fear is fear itself.' It is also an excellent idea never to say anything mean."

"I know." Scott was looking down at his feet, feeling embarrassed. "I really feel wicked after I say horrible things."

"Right, Scott, remember when you were so angry you said you hated every-one, even your mom and Joey?"

Scott hung his head, "I didn't really mean it."

"Perhaps not," Relato swirled his scepter creating a flicker of light that appeared and disappeared, "but it stays as negative energy until you cancel it out. Negatives have to be crossed off the record in the Book of Life, and the sooner, the better—but better late than never. It can work even years later, like forgiveness."

"What should I do?" Scott rolled his eyes and shrugged his shoulders in frustration. "I don't really hate Joey; he just drives me nuts."

"There you go again!" Relato raised his right hand firmly to signify "stop" and gently placed his left hand on Scott's shoulder as he explained. "No one ever drives you nuts, you allow it to happen. Think—that's what you should do—think! You are responsible for your own thoughts and actions."

Relato led Scott to a chair. "Let me tell you a story about a Mind/Bodybuilder in one of my lectures. This vivacious youngster stood up in the middle of class and blurted out his thoughts on 'thoughts.'"

Relato mimicked the boy as he told the story. "The boy placed his hands on his temples and then threw his hand down as if to pitch a ball at his feet while announcing to the class, 'If I can think it, then I can sink it. I call these bad thoughts—my STINK'N THINK'N.'"

Scott burst out laughing. "I would love to go to one of your classes. That boy sounds really smart."

"Well, maybe that can be arranged," Relato winked. "That is one of my favorite stories about teaching our youth who become pretty confident and creative with their wisdom, I might add. I can see it happening to you already."

"I wish I could sink it, and get rid of my STINK'N THINK'N," Scott sighed longingly.

"You must learn to live consciously." Relato exclaimed. "You saw how different things were in 'Future Flash' when you were nice to Joey and shared your computer. You made him your friend, not your enemy."

"Yes, but how do I do that all the

time?" Scott shrugged his shoulders, feeling perplexed.

"You do it one incident at a time by being alert and aware, and using your conscience."

"I don't get it." Scott leaned forward in his chair, put his head in his hands in deep thought, and replied helplessly, "What is my conscience?"

Relato reached his hand out and gently patted Scott on the head. "Your conscience is your brain's inner monitor of what is right and what is wrong. And it's always urging you to do the right thing. Do you think that the next time Joey starts to bother you that you could do what you did on the path that was strewn with glass?"

"What do you mean?" Scott's brain was spinning with all these new concepts as he straightened out of his slumping posture to look up at Relato.

"Do you think you could step back and think about what will happen if you answer him with a nasty remark? You would not step on the broken glass, but would choose to go around it, taking the path that would not hurt you."

"I guess so," he hesitantly agreed, though still puzzled.

"What do you think you should do to avoid a fight?"

Scott's face lit up. "I know! I'll tell him a joke to get him to laugh, and then ask him to play a game. Is that the kind of stuff you mean?"

"Precisely!" Relato exclaimed, raising his scepter as a sign of victory, delighted that Scott was finally grasping the principles. "That sounds like a step in the right direction. If you learn to control your temper you'll feel better about yourself. And if you help others to control their tempers, they will feel better about themselves. You will be developing positive attitudes and making friends instead of enemies."

"That sounds easy," Scott agreed, "but

I think it will be hard to do."

"Just try the friendly, cooperative approach with Joey the next time, and you will find with each successful episode it will get easier to do. Soon you will look back and wonder why you two didn't get along before. If you become more aware of what's going on around you, then your deposits into the Inner National Bank of Worth will far outnumber the withdrawals sending your Growth Fund off the charts."

Scott stood up, holding a withdrawal slip, and ripped it up saying, "No more STINK'N THINK'N!" He was having so much fun that he laughed and joined in as Relato sang ...

When I Laugh
Performed by Grandmaster Melle Mel

When I laugh, it makes me happy
even if I were sad - when I laugh.
If I was brutal, laughing makes me
feel glad - when I laugh.

It helps me realize that nothing's so
bad - when I laugh.

Now everybody get closer maybe
you'll see alright,
And smile because everything will be
alright,
And laugh when you work or play,
And remember tomorrow you can
finish what you started today.
And even though things don't work out,
Keep a positive mind, that's what
happiness is all about,
Because today what didn't work out,
Is something tomorrow, we'll sit
around and laugh about.

When I laugh - it makes me happy
even if I were sad - when I laugh.
If I was brutal, laughing makes me
feel glad - when I laugh.
It helps me realize that nothing's so
bad - when I laugh.

And let me tell ya, I know your pain; I
feel your grief,

But come on y'all give me a smile, let me see those teeth.
Things are never are as bad as they seem.
Greet life and treat life like it's a bowl of ice cream;
You take it one scoop at a time.
Learn from your mistakes, find something new to do with your mind.
Take your time, don't act fast.
And whenever I'm lost, I get on the right Path - when I laugh.
I feel somethin' comin'over me,
A good something all over me - when I laugh.
All my friends are close to me,
And that's how it's supposed to be - when I laugh.
I start feelin' real good inside,
Like everything's gonna be alright - when I laugh.

Put your hands up, put your hands up.
Come on.
Everything's gonna be alright.

Everything, everything's gonna be alright.
Everything, everything's gonna be alright.
When I laugh. Oh yeah.
Smile for me, baby.

☆   ☆   ☆

Chapter 10. Escape from Angroid and Graboid

"I have a question for you," Relato said as he walked with Scott into another magnificent room.

The library was like a church, with high shelves of ancient volumes that held between their covers the wisdom of the ages.

Bright chandeliers hung in a row from the arched stone ceilings, and their footsteps echoed as they walked.

"Wow," Scott gasped. "Look at all these books."

"We make it mandatory that all Cortex children have way more books than toys," Relato responded. Scott found that incredi-

These magical books hold the wisdom
of the ages, past, present and future,
where you are free to travel through
their pages.

ble. "Someday I will show you our music library. It is really quite extraordinary." Scott was dumbfounded.

"What do you think about Graboid?" Relato asked as they strolled across the vast room of books.

"Huh?" Scott snapped out of his star-struck daze.

"Do you ever have a problem with your brother and your toys?"

"All the time," Scott admitted, irritated at the memory. "I don't like him playing with my things. He breaks them. Well mostly, he just grabs and runs off, and throws them under his bed."

"Sounds like Graboid, doesn't it?" Relato asked. Even though he knew the answer, he wanted to hear Scott's opinion. "And does it seem to get worse around Christmas or birthdays when new toys come into the house?"

"It sure does," Scott groaned, remembering their fights. "But what am I supposed to do? Let him have everything he wants?"

"No," exclaimed Relato as he walked toward a huge oak desk. "That would give him another wrong idea. But because you're older it's up to you to figure out ahead of time how to handle him. It's only natural for Joey to want to play with new toys. You can suggest something else to do. That's what you did in 'Future Flash,' remember? Surely your mom has told you to share, to take turns, and to play nicely."

"Yeah, but it doesn't always work."

"I know it's not easy," said Relato as he squatted down to Scott's level, placing his hands gently on Scott's shoulders, and looking him right in the eyes. "But think about choices, think about the Path. It's a challenge, but remember, it's not Joey you want to control, but yourself and the situation.

"First you have to control yourself to keep out Angroid," Relato reminded Scott. "Then you have to handle the situation."

Relato stood up and continued walking to his desk. "The way you play together is called interaction. If you and Joey change your attitudes to cooperation instead of competition, you will have much more fun growing up."

Turning back to Scott he said with deep conviction, "You need each other. Learning to get along with people is the most important job you have. When you're successful at that, it's called brotherhood, and you have the best opportunity to practice it with Joey."

"Now I think I get it," said Scott, beaming, as Sitara entered the room. "It's like a chain reaction starting with your family and friends, then people at your school, then people at your work, and finally the whole world."

"Precisely, Scott! Always remember that if your family is strained with multiple dysfunctions, you must choose other junctions. We know that congeniality will bind friends of like mind," Relato responded. "Don't forget, as Shakespeare wrote many years ago, 'One touch of nature makes the world kin.'"

Relato walked over to greet Sitara and they all started to sing…

World Family Tree
Performed by Grandmaster Melle Mel Featuring Lady Gaga

Family tree, love, love your roots.
Family tree.
If you love your mother please tell her that you love her.
And don't forget to tell your brother and don't miss your sis,
Amidst all this family bliss -
And give your mom a big hug and a kiss.
Kind words go a long way, write a song today,
And you might stop someone from going the wrong way.
Don't delay, it's my advice think twice and be nice.
You just might save a life.

Just one life, is just like saving the world.
It's more than wealth, it's just like saving yourself.
The family tree, love your roots. And if we all
Follow suit, then we can begin to bear fruit.

We're gonna make a pact and
Stop at the roots and take it back,
We all need a family. Oh.
Family tree, love, love your roots.
Family tree.

It takes a village to raise a child.
It might take the whole world just to save a child.
And one of the children just might save the world.
So we need every boy and girl -
And we all need to walk in the same path stride for stride,
With hearts and arms open wide,
With the same kind of mind,

With a true love divine,
And never let the blind lead the blind.
And never have no fear be a voice
for the deaf to hear.
Spread the word so the voiceless
one's can be heard.
Build a road where even the lame can
roam free.
For you and me,
A new world family tree.

We're gonna make a pact and
Stop at the roots and take it back,
We all need a family. Oh.
Family tree, love, love your roots.
Family tree.

Sisters and brothers may attack you,
But stop to think, why do what they
do,
Just think first, never burst,
Or you'll find out, that you're only
making things worse.
A little louder now.
(Repeat 3 times)

We're gonna make a pact and
Stop at the roots and take it back,
We all need a family. Oh.
Family tree love. love your roots.
Family tree.

Brothers and sisters fill your life with
happiness and harmony,
And just follow me and the whole
world will be your family tree.
PEACE!

Chapter 11. Biofitness Fun

Relato led Scott outside. On a wide
lawn were fields for running and jumping,
great gravel tracks for racing, bars for climbing, and a bright, still, sunlit pool shimmering beneath viewing stands and a throne.
Scott had never seen anything like this in all
his life. The swimming pool was long with

head rotation

front ... **then side**

elbow on opposite side

stretch looking up

shoulder roll ... **with body twist**

front kick

diagonal kick

upper body twist

elbow to opposite knee

touch toes legs together

kick with a hop

hop reaching up

jumping jack

crab

twist and jump

lower body twist and jump

reach opposite toes

sit up

twisting jump

stomach crunch

legs apart don't bounce

Activity not Passivity: It doesn't take long to make yourself strong.

water laps of multiple colors. The climbing bars formed a fifty-foot bronze mountain of lattice sculpture with safety ropes hanging from every peak.

The fields were sectioned off and manicured for every specific sport. At one end of the field was an enormous building of stone with two central pillars encompassing the field in a semicircle with many windows and rooms. There were gargoyles carved into the arched entrance between the two pillars. As they moved closer Scott read the engraving across the enormous mahogany doors: "The Biorhythm Academy." And underneath in smaller letters: "Carpe Diem."

Scott shouted with excitement, "So this is the school! And that must be its motto — 'Seize the Day.'" He was proud of knowing that little bit of Latin.

Relato laughed. "Yes, this is where the greatest minds of all time share their wisdom." Relato wanted Scott to appreciate the connection between exercise and emotions. "Exercise is another excellent way to fight depressed feelings. A physical body workout builds endorphins in the brain."

"What are endorphins?" Scott asked with a bewildered look. He was learning so many new terms!

"Endorphins are hormones that the brain releases into the bloodstream to circulate through the body to stimulate it in a positive way. They affect your emotions and lift you up in both body and spirit. They give you a better feeling about yourself and the world. That's why endorphins are called mood elevators. They are the body's natural stress reliever. It all has to do with nature. Once you know how your body works, you can make it work for you."

Scott looked mystified. He wondered what kind of exercises could raise a person's mood. "Is that what the Mind/Body-builders were doing in the meadow when I saw them perform strange movements with their arms and legs?"

"Precisely!" Relato affirmed, pleased that Scott had made the connection. He lunged forward into a training stance to demonstrate. "That was the special Biofitness workout—part of our daily routine. You see, here in Cortex, we believe very strongly in both mental fitness and bodily fitness. We do not consider exercise work; it's a training program, a wonderful learning experience, not a job."

Scott nodded, but was still perplexed.

"Anger creates negative tension," Relato ex-plained. "Exercise is how we create positive tension to balance the energy flow, and reverse it to positive energy again. Negative tension is just another way of saying, 'Welcome, Angroid.' If he takes over, he spoils your happiness, and Joey's, even your Mom and Dad's, or any person's you are interacting with. Don't forget that your body and your attitudes are interwoven. Anger makes the body tense. Happiness makes it relax. Biofitness exercises relax both the body and the mind."

"I still don't get it." Scott scratched his head with a befuddled look.

"I'll prove it to you." Relato made a mean face. "Look at me. I am angry and I'm frowning at you. How does that make you feel?"

Scott shrank back. "Mad, sad, and a little scared. It makes me feel as if you don't like me."

"Precisely!" Realto then made a pleasant face. "Now look at me, I am smiling and saying I like you, and I think we will have fun together. How does that make you feel?"

"Wow!" Scott straightened up and beamed with delight. "That makes me feel better, I'm smiling too, and I feel happier. This is amazing!"

Relato smiled. "Now you're starting to understand the key to a peaceful and fit mind, body, and spirit. I'm going to let you in on a Cortex state secret." He made a show of looking left and right, then, leaning over to Scott's ear he cupped a hand to the side of his mouth and whispered. "It is the holistic structure of our education system implemented through the Biorhythm Academy that provides a very peaceful and healthy society here on Cortex. Through language, which is right brain activity, and music which is left brain activity, we are able to balance our learning and the development of our EQ, PQ, and IQ."

Scott nodded that he thought he understood.

Relato straightened up and explained further in a confident voice. "We must grow strong physically as well as mentally. I watch over my Cortex Rescue Team so they don't let any Viroids take over. Viroids especially like to go after children, but they can go after adults too. We have daily exercise training as part of our mind, body, and emotional fitness programs. We call it the Biofitness Club. Biofitness is when you tighten your muscles in a particular position and hold them there for a few seconds while you move in a controlled, slow motion dance. This develops good posture and strengthens the core muscles. It is also known as body shaping. Your posture and your breathing are important in keeping your mind alert. For example, have you ever felt tired while sitting in school and not able to concentrate, and then fallen into a slumped position?"

"Sure, by third or fourth period I can't concentrate at all," Scott shrugged. "I kind of go into a daydream sometimes."

"Well," Relato nodded, "you are not meant to sit completely still for such a long period of time. When you fall into a slumped posture, this compromises the oxygen in your body making you tired. Occasionally, you need to adjust your posture expanding your chest, and take some deep breaths to rejuvenate yourself." Relato stood very straight and inhaled air through his nose. "If you roll your shoulders back, hold your head up, and take in a deep breath when you feel tired, it will bring the oxygen to your brain and muscles making you alert.

Then, you will be able to concentrate much better. Try it, and you will see that it makes all the difference."

"So that's why I get tired." Scott straightened his posture and held his head high. Copying Relato's breathing, he expelled a gust of air through his mouth. "Boy, that really woke me up and made me feel better. There are a lot of things I have to learn about my body that affect my energy level."

Relato raised his scepter and smiled in agreement. "Precisely! I would say you have learned a lot in a short time. But remember that learning never stops with age or time. Now you are beginning to connect your experiences." As he sat down next to Scott, Relato formed a circle with the light from his scepter. Inside the circle, the hologram TV screen flickered on again. The Cortex Mind/Bodybuilders who had saved Scott were seen in the meadow doing their exercise routine.

"Would you like to join them, Scott?" Relato asked.

"Awesome," Scott radiated excitement.

Relato stood up, raised his scepter with the attached screen and in one curving motion of his arm, swept the screen through Scott, instantly depositing him in the meadow with the Mind/Bodybuilders.

As Scott happily joins their routine they are suddenly attacked by the Viroids. This time Scott is not afraid. He sees Angroid and takes off after him, chasing him past the flowers and along the bank of the stream that borders the meadow. Scott is gaining on Angroid and almost catches him, but Angroid makes a sharp turn and disappears into the woods. Scott tries to stop his momentum and teeters on the edge of the bank. In that moment, he realizes that if he had done more exercises he'd have better control of his balance — then falls into the water.

Scott spins through a dark tunnel and is ejected out into bright daylight. He finds himself in knee-deep water furiously splashing and flailing his arms and legs. Looking up, he sees Eli and Angelina on the bridge.

Scott had returned through the same portal, transcending space and time, he landed back in the exact moment he had left. To his friends watching from the bridge, only a few seconds had elapsed. Rubbing a small bump on his head as he climbs out of the water, he says, "What happened?"

His mother runs up as he comes out of the stream, dripping wet. Who is Relato? Scott wonders to himself. This was more than a dream; it was a dream with a meaningful message I will never forget.

He tries to do some of the martial moves he remembers the Mind/Bodybuilders doing to show Eli and Angelina. "Mom, can't we stay here for an exercise session? I want to build myself up."

His mother, looking relieved says,

"You're soaking wet! What happened? Are you sure you're okay?" When Scott continues to exercise, she takes him by the hand and says, "I'm happy that you want to exercise, but let's wait until tomorrow. We have to get you home and dry before you catch cold. Today has been exciting enough!"

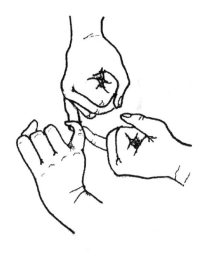

Scott looks at his mother and thinks, You don't know how exciting my day has been!

The next morning, when Scott wakes up, he finds a CD glowing with an amazing light sitting on his desk, and a mysterious little wooden box with intricate carvings of the Mind/Body-builders. As he touches the disc, his body feels a surge of positive energy and overall warmth.

Eli, Angelina, and his little brother,

Joey, arrive just as he is putting the glowing disc into his CD player. Scott swears them all to secrecy as he shows them the box containing an Inner National Bank of Worth transaction sheet. They huddle together and lock pinkies, to make their secret pact.

To their amazement, they are all able to easily follow the Biofitness routine, and as the music begins, they all sing ...

Activity-Not Passivity
Performed by Grandmaster Melle Mel

Activity not passivity, come on,
activity not passivity.
Listen to the sound, spread it all
around.
Come on y'all get down, now were
gonna show you how.
We got that activity, not passivity,
come on, activity not passivity,
Listen to the sound, spread it all
around.

I'm sure you'll agree that it's easy as
ONE, TWO, THREE.

Put your hands up, now everybody
put your hands down,
Now everybody spin your body around,
We gonna do some knee bends and
jumpin' jacks,
And when we're done we're gonna let
you know its fun to react.
With foresight and hindsight get your
mind right.
Wealth is when you see your inner
self, with your eyesight.
Confidence, get yourself together,
Don't let your life be measured by the
peer pressure.

Come on activity not passivity, come
on, activity not passivity.
Listen to the sound, spread it all around.
Come on ya all get down, now were
gonna show you how.
We got that activity, not passivity.
Come on, activity not passivity.

Listen to the sound, spread it all around.
I'm sure you'll agree that it's easy as
ONE, TWO, THREE.

It don't take long to make yourself
strong, sing along.
We can do it together with the energy
song.
Must be tenacious, repel the
rapacious.
No need to be vicious, don't be
bodacious.
Always be gracious, get yourself a
program, man,
And wave your hands from side to side.
Pack your bags, life is a ride.
Have self-pride, don't be a bigot.
Let me kick it,
And make the right moves.
You can write your own ticket. Uhh.

Activity not passivity, come on,
activity not passivity,
Listen to the sound, spread it all around,
Come on ya all get down, now were

gonna show you how.
We got that activity, not passivity.
Come on, activity not passivity.
Listen to that sound, spread it all around,
I'm sure you'll agree that it's easy as
ONE, TWO, THREE.

Don't be passive, don't be shy.
Don't be afraid to ask why, don't be
scared to try.
Mankind was designed to explore the
universe,
Starburst you gotta know yourself first.
Knowledge starts with you and ends
with us all.
Don't ever be afraid to fall.
It doesn't matter how many times you
fall, y'all, that's what's up;
We only count the amount of times
you get back up.

Now, come on activity not passivity,
come on, activity not passivity.
Listen to the sound, spread it all
around.

Come on ya all get down, now were
gonna show you how.
We got that activity, not passivity.
Come on, activity not passivity.
Listen to that sound, spread it all around.
I'm sure you'll agree that it's easy as
ONE, TWO, THREE.

Work your body, work your body,
And make sure you don't hurt nobody.
Come on.
Uhh, hey.

The End

Inner National Bank of Worth

Deposits

A - Activity
B - Biofitness
C - Cooperation
D - Devotion
E - Effort
F - Fearlessness
G - Goodness
H - Honesty
I - Imagination
J - Joyfulness/Happiness
K - Kindness
L - Listen
M - Modesty
N - Nutrition
O - Openmindedness
P - Positive Attitude
Q - Quietude
R - Respect
S - Self-esteem
T - Think
U - Understanding
V - Veritas
W - Wisdom
X - X-cellence
Y - Yielding
Z - Zippy

Withdrawals

a - anger
b - bullying
c - critical
d - dishonesty
e - envy
f - fighting
g - greed/selfishness
h - horrible
i - impatience
j - jealousy
k - kicking
l - lying
m - mad
n - nagging
o - offensive
p - passivity
q - quitter
r - revenge
s - swearing
t - temper
u - uncaring
v - violent
w - worry
x - aggeration
y - yelling
z - zombie

Inner National Bank of Worth

<u>Deposits</u>

A – Activity: The quality of being active, of exerting energy and using normal mental or bodily power. Being lively. Do you take time to think and act and play physical games rather than just sit at the computer playing games?

B – Biofitness: This type of exercising will help ensure that the body distributes inhaled oxygen to muscle tissue during the increased physical effort. You need to strengthen your core muscles. Even if you do only four or five shapes a day it will help. Do you make time every day to do your Biofitness exercises?

C – Cooperation: Working or acting together for a common purpose or benefit. People working with others willingly and agreeably. Do you help around the house and in school without having to be asked?

D – Devotion: Earnest dedication to a cause. Have faith and trust in what you believe. Are you devoted or dedicated to good causes?

E – Effort: Exertion of your physical or mental powers. You do something by hard work, or extra effort. There are two types of effort; 1) Physical effort — take out the trash, clean your room, and give your parents or your sister or brother a hug. 2) Emotional effort — say nice things to your sister or brother or friends in school. Spend some time with, or just compliment someone who is bullied in school. After awhile your effort will become effortless. Do you make the effort?

F – Fearlessness: Without fear; bold; spirited; brave; heroic; gallant. Developing the courage to stand by your positive qualities, and thinking about good things are two ways to combat your fears. Fears hold you back from being you. Are you being courageous in your life?

G – Goodness: Being kind to others plus being moral and virtuous. Do you have an attitude of always wanting to be kind and helpful?

H – Honesty: The quality of being truthful, sincere, and fair. Are you fair to others and do you command the same respect back?

I – Imagination: The ability to form mental images or concepts of things not actually present to the senses. Expand your talents and be creative: invent, fantasize, mold, shape, conceptualize, think up, dream up, and be productive. Are you being original and being all you can be?

J – Joyfulness: Showing or causing happiness and delight. Do you try to make others happy? Are you kind and friendly?

K – Kindness: The quality of being nice and being friendly to others. Kindness lets others know that you care about them. How kind are you being?

L – Listen: The ability to pay attention and understand what another is saying. You should hear, focus, and learn. Do you listen attentively?

M – Modesty: The quality of being free from vanity and boastfulness, and having a regard for decency of behavior and speech. Are you being a good person without needing to brag about how good you are?

N – Nutrition: Learning the best things to eat and drink to help you to grow and be healthy. You will compromise your energy and your power levels if you eat an unhealthy diet. Do you eat and drink the proper things?

O – Openmindedness: Being receptive to new ideas; unprejudiced; unbiased; impartial. Is your mind open to new ideas?

P – Positive Attitude: Emphasizing what

is hopeful, good, or constructive. Are you happy and hopeful in your outlook?

Q – Quietude: The state of staying calm and still. Working on self-control. It is a true art to be able to rest, relax, and restore yourself. Do you take time to simply think?

R – Respect: The art of showing consideration, appreciation, courtesy, thoughtfulness, high regard, and high opinion to others. How much do you respect others?

S – Self-esteem: Having a realistic or favorable impression of yourself; self-respect. You maintain pride and self-reliance. Self-confidence, self-respect, and independence form the powerful shield against anyone breaking you down or abusing you. How high is your self-esteem?

T – Think: To employ one's mind remembering experiences and making rational decisions. Do you step back and think before you act?

U – Understanding: Trying to grasp ideas and the true meaning of things. Do you think things out before you decide what they mean? Do you try to understand others?

V - Veritas: The Latin word for truth; reality; the real world. Do you try to grasp the truth about things, and the reality of situations?

W – Wisdom: Knowing what is true or right coupled with good judgment as to action; intelligence; insight. Do you try to make wise decisions?

X – X-cellence: Excellence, the state of doing extremely well. Being all that you can be. Do you work hard to succeed?

Y – Yielding: Inclined to be objective under pressure. Being flexible and not always demanding your own way. Are you able to go with the flow?

Z – Zippy: To be lively and peppy. Do you often smile and try to spread a happy, positive attitude?

Withdrawals

a – anger: Strong feelings of displeasure and belligerence. Do you become angry easily? Are you in a constant state of irritation, annoyance, or even rage? There are two types of anger.

1) Provoked anger — When you lose

your cool, become irritated or annoyed, and take something that does not belong to you, or say something mean to your sister or brother, schoolmates, or parents. Sometimes really losing it and getting out of control or enraged, escalating your anger to the point of physical violence (hitting, pushing, and fighting).

2) Reactive anger — This is when somebody else (your sister, brother, friends, and yes, even your parents exhibit reactive anger) loses his or her cool and takes your things, or says something mean to you, and you respond back with anger or rage — now, everybody is angry. This is the worst and is the most difficult to control. It forms a chain reaction of anger that keeps spreading. Do you find it difficult to step back, gain your composure, and change your reaction to a positive action — thus gaining control, and changing the situation?

b – bullying: A bully is habitually cruel to others who are weaker; whether it is on a physical level — punching and fighting — or an emotional level — name calling and degrading someone's differences (skin color, religion, culture, personal looks or deformities). You must know that the real weakness is in the attitude of the bully not the victim. So step back and think before you badger your sister or brother, pester your parents, fight your foes, tease your friends, annoy your teacher, torment, bother or harass anyone. Do you have trouble staying in control and trying to keep the peace?

c – critical: Inclined to find fault or to judge with severity, often too readily. Do you constantly find things to complain about? If you are disapproving and faultfinding you might end up with no friends. Is it hard for you to stop and think before you complain about someone?

d – dishonesty: One who is disposed to lie, cheat, or steal; not worthy of trust or belief. Are you not a person who can be believed and counted on to do the correct thing?

e – envy: You become resentful or mad at the happiness or joy of someone else. For example, if your friend wins a race and you do not, can you still be gracious and genuinely happy for him or her? Can you compete with yourself, not with others?

f – fighting: You should avoid all possible forms of physical attack. Fighting usually starts verbally, so it's best to control yourself. Can you stop and think how to reverse the situation?

g – greed/selfishness: You have a strong

desire, a piggishness for things. You are never satisfied because you want more toys, more food, more money, more clothes. This can be more serious when it leads to envy and stealing. In the case of food it can lead to obesity. Is it difficult for you to set limits and boundaries for yourself?

h – horrible: Being extremely unpleasant. Do you ever try to frighten anyone? Do you behave in a manner that makes others afraid of you?

i – impatience: Not accepting delay, opposition, or pain with calmness. Being intolerant. Do you ever become angry because you have to wait for something? Do you ever cry when you are hurt even though the pain isn't really that bad?

j – jealousy: Resentment against another's success or advantage. Do you ever get angry when someone gets something and you don't?

k – kicking: To strike with your foot or feet. Do you ever kick or punch others in anger?

l – lying: Providing false information. Being untruthful when you know better. Do you ever say that you did not do something when you really did do it?

m – mad: To become enraged, greatly provoked, or irritated. Do you ever become angry just to get your way, or to show displeasure?

n – nagging: To find fault or complain in an irritating or relentless manner. Do you ever whine and complain to annoy your parents until you get your way?

o – offensive: Causing displeasure. Being irritating and annoying; attacking. Have you ever hit someone or been mean to try and prove something?

p – passivity: The state or condition of not reacting visibly to something that should produce signs of emotions or feelings. Do you just ignore some things that you feel bad about? Do you act as if important things don't matter?

q – quitter: A person who gives up too easily, especially in the face of some difficulty. For example, have you ever stayed home from school just because it was raining?

r – revenge: To exact punishment for a perceived wrong. To retaliate to gain satisfaction for something wrong you felt was done to you. Do you ever try to get back at people you feel have offended you?

s – swearing: To use profane or bad language. Do you ever use bad language—either because you're irritated or to show off?

t – temper: Heat of mind or passion shown in outbursts of anger or resentment. Do you "lose it" and make a big fuss when something gets you angry?

u – uncaring: Unkempt; neglect; disheveled; messy. Do you allow yourself and your room to look messy and neglected? Is your homework sloppy?

v – violent: Swift and intense use of physical force. Do you often fight or yell to get what you want?

w – worry: To suffer from disturbing thoughts. Do you become anxious, and sit fretting instead of playing and exercising?

x – x-aggeration: Exaggeration. To overstate and magnify things beyond the limits of truth. This is another form of lying. Do you ever blow things out of proportion to make yourself look better?

y – yelling: To cry out or speak with a strong, loud voice; to shout. Do you ever yell just to get attention when it is not necessary?

z – zombie: A person whose behavior or responses are wooden, listless, or seemingly rote. Do you ever act as if you just don't care about anything or anyone?

In order to become a member of the Cortex Club, which is a branch of the Biorhythm Academy, you must start now to accumulate lots of cents, which indicate you are growing in maturity (sense). You must eliminate the chips which make you bloated with negative attitude and STINK'N THINK'N.

It is simple to start. Just make copies of the blank transaction sheet and follow the directions.

Inner National Bank of Worth
Weekly Transaction Sheet

Month_____ Year____
Name_____
Account#_____

	Monday	Tuesday	Wednesday	Thursday	Friday	Saturday	Sunday
Deposits #of cents							

Total cents _____ _____ _____ _____ _____ _____ _____ _____

Total chips _____ _____ _____ _____ _____ _____ _____ _____

Total net worth for the week =

Make copies of this sheet and fill in your name, the month, the year and your account number. Put the date at the top of each column for each day of the week. Use Scott's transaction sheet as an example. Then go to the glossary and jot down the first letter of the action you performed, and how many times you repeated it. Total these daily and then weekly. You must end

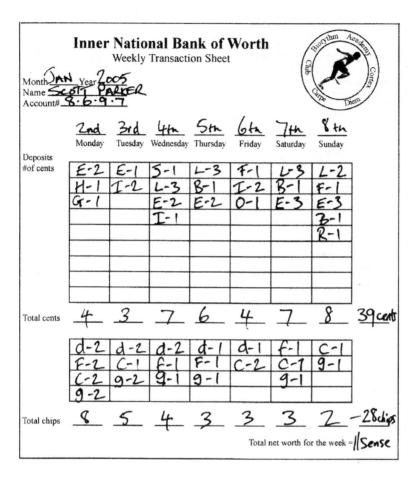

Inner National Bank of Worth
Weekly Transaction Sheet

Month JAN Year 2005
Name SCOTT PARKER
Account# 8·6·9·7

	2nd Monday	3rd Tuesday	4th Wednesday	5th Thursday	6th Friday	7th Saturday	8th Sunday	
Deposits #of cents	E-2	E-1	S-1	L-3	F-1	L-3	L-2	
	H-1	I-2	L-3	B-1	I-2	B-1	F-1	
	G-1		E-2	E-2	O-1	E-3	E-3	
			I-1				B-1	
							R-1	
Total cents	4	3	7	6	4	7	8	39 cents
	d-2	d-2	d-2	d-1	d-1	f-1	C-1	
	F-2	C-1	f-1	F-1	C-2	C-1	9-1	
	C-2	9-2	9-1	9-1		9-1		
	9-2							
Total chips	8	5	4	3	3	3	2	-28 chips

Total net worth for the week = //Sense

up with more deposits than withdrawals to achieve a positive result.

If you get those chips off your shoulder and develop a positive attitude, you will mature and grow in sense as your account grows in cents. You must end up with more deposits than withdrawals to achieve a positive result.

Grandmaster Melle Mel grew up in the Bronx utilizing his creative musical talents and lyrical genius to become successful. Melle Mel, a three-time Grammy winner and one of the pioneers of hip-hop is most noted for his all-time classic song "The Message," to which Rolling Stone magazine gave a rare five-star review.

Melle's original style changed music and laid the foundation for what has become an exploding musical culture. He was a contributing author for Q: The Autobiography of Quincy Jones. An article in the BBC News listed Melle Mel as the single greatest rapper of all time.

He has been nominated to be inducted into the Rock 'n' Roll Hall of Fame. He has a physique to match his verbal firepower, a world-class bodybuilder and competes regularly. He now has a new "Message" to all the children of the world.

You can read 'n' rap along with Grandmaster Melle Mel and the characters as they speak and sing the complete text and seven original inspirational songs of hip-hop and pop. Melle brings lyrical dexterity and his trade-mark delivery elevating children's records way above the standard, into something with more substance and a positive message. The Portal in the Park is in a league of its own.

Cricket Casey is a motivator and educator in the field of mind-body fitness.

She is a graduate of New York University, with a degree in physical therapy, and she holds a degree in biopsychology from William Paterson University.

In private practice, she has worked as a physical therapist, personal trainer, and, life coach. For many years she served as a therapist in the New York City public schools and various private preschools. Casey has produced four fitness videos and a children's book which have been distributed nationally and cited in numerous newspapers and magazines including the National Physical Therapy Bulletin and the Wall Street Journal.

She also developed a Biofitness Training program for kids to stretch and strengthen proximal core muscles sprouting beautiful posture. She is presently working on a wellness training program and developing an ergonomic design to create a more productive setting in the classroom. Manhattan is her office and the subway is her car. Casey is always seeking out the next opportunity.

Everyone associated with this book she encountered on the street, in the subway or in a café. She is a firm believer in team effort and together, Melle and Casey make slam dunk talent. The Portal in the Park is the first in a multimedia book series for the multitasking generation.

Movin' On!

Proof

Made in the USA
Charleston, SC
14 January 2016